COME MEET DRAYDEN

BY DANA YOUNG-ASKEW
ILLUSTRATED BY CAMERON WILSON

Drayden is our brother. We want to introduce you to him. Come meet Drayden.

Say hi to our brother Drayden.

He may not respond but he hears you. He is an awesome listener.

Our brother spins around in a circle. He spins around and around so fast. He is pretty wiggly too. You will always see Drayden moving. His movements make him feel good.

Drayden does not like our morning or bedtime routine. We have to help him brush his teeth, wash his face and even change his clothes.

He enjoys playing in the water. Any water he can find. A pool, bathtub or even a sink! Most of the time, he splashes excessively. Water gets everywhere. Splash, splash, splash!

Even though we all love birthday parties, Drayden does not.

Parties are too loud. They have too many people. Events are just no fun for him. Sometimes we even have to leave early.

Our brother loves plain cheese pizza. Applesauce and cheeseburgers are some of his favorite foods too. Drayden does not always eat his vegetables or fruits so we make sure he takes his vitamins to keep him healthy.

Drayden copies whatever you say. We like to think of it as an echo.

You can find Drayden repeating the last thing you said to him.

At playtime, you will find that Drayden rather play alone. He has fun lining up things by color, size and shape. Drayden is very responsible with his toys. He takes care of them. All of his toys are special to him.

Drayden goes to a different school than us. Mom says they are able to give him the special help he needs. A school, teacher and bus fit just for him. We are able to help Mom get Drayden off his bus in the evenings.

There are times Drayden gets upset. We do not know what is bothering him. There is not always a way we can help. Therefore, we clear out a space for him to safely cry. We lay with Drayden. When he is feeling better, we all hug him tight.

Our brother is a terrific reader. He knows so many words. Drayden likes to read aloud. All of us gather around to listen to him read. Reading together is one of our favorite activities to do.

When we watch television with Drayden, he changes the channel in the middle of the program. He will rewind a show to watch the same parts repeatedly.

We teach Drayden new things. Drayden teaches us new things too. We make space in our lives for Drayden. Drayden is our brother. We love Drayden just the way he is!

CPSIA information can be obtained
at www.ICGtesting.com
Printed in the USA
LVHW060945150121
676552LV00002B/5